Kids...
Choose You...

"When I figure... the back, I almost exploded!"

Sophia DeSanto, age 9

"I read them because they are interesting, and they have lots of cool titles and words to use."

Laini Ribera, age 9

"There can be at least 28 ENDINGS in it and so many choices. Other books you have to read the whole book in order, well not this one!"

August Backman, age 10

"I like that you can choose. So, if you want to choose something, you can do it."

Colin Lawrence, age 10

"The CYOA books are crazy because there are so many crazy choices."

Isaiah Sparkes, age 12

CHOOSE YOUR OWN ADVENTURE®

THE LOST NINJA

BY JAY LEIBOLD

ILLUSTRATED BY SUZANNE NUGENT
COVER ILLUSTRATED BY GABHOR UTOMO

CHOOSECO
WAITSFIELD, VERMONT

Book design: Stacey Boyd, Big Eyedea Visual Design

For information regarding permission, write to:

CHOOSECO
P.O. Box 46, Waitsfield, Vermont 05673
www.cyoa.com

Publisher's Cataloging-In-Publication Data
Names: Leibold, Jay, author. | Nugent, Suzanne, illustrator. | Utomo,
Gabhor, illustrator.
Title: The lost ninja / by Jay Leibold ; interior artwork by Suzanne
Nugent ; cover artwork by Gabhor Utomo.
Other Titles: Choose your own adventure.
Description: [Revised edition]. | Waitsfield, Vermont : Chooseco,
[2019] | Originally published: New York : Bantam Books, ©1991. Choose
your own adventure ; 113. | Interest age level: 009-012. | Summary:
"You trained in Japan to become a powerful ninja, and now your skills
are needed in San Francisco. You are far from the magical dojo you
once called home. But has the dojo's strange curse followed you into
your new life? You recognize ruthless gangsters you've crossed paths
with before. Did they follow you here? You hear rumors that priceless
antiques are making their way along the same route you just traveled--
will the thefts be blamed on you?"--Provided by publisher.
Identifiers: ISBN 1-937133-35-4 | ISBN 978-1-937133-35-1
Subjects: LCSH: Ninja--California--San Francisco--Juvenile fiction. |
Gangsters--Juvenile fiction. | CYAC: Ninja--California--San Francisco-
-Juvenile fiction. | Gangsters--Fiction. | LCGFT: Action and adventure
fiction. | Choose-your-own stories.
Classification: LCC PZ7.L53276 Lo 2019 | DDC [Fic]--dc23

SPECIAL NOTE ON THE *NINJA*

The ancient art of *ninjutsu* was developed in the eleventh and twelfth centuries by Japanese mountain clans. Drawing on their knowledge of martial arts, war tactics, and mystical practices—especially those practiced in a branch of Buddhism known in Japan as *shugendo*—they passed their art from one generation to the next.

According to legend, mountain creatures called *tengu* first taught the *ninja* their art. They also taught them *kuji* (sorcery) and how to use mystic finger positions to channel energy, key into the underlying forces of the universe, and alter the fabric of space and time.

Each *ryu* (tradition or school) has its own specializations and secrets, which are taught by a *sensei* (master or teacher) at the *dojo* (the place where martial arts are practiced). A student of *ninjutsu* will learn techniques of empty-hand combat, the use of weapons and special devices, as well as tactics of escape, deception, and invisibility, and the strategies of espionage, attack, and defense.

In this book, YOU are a modern-day *ninja*. You must bring your *ninja* training from Japan to the aid of a classmate in the United States. Defending a friend you trust is difficult, but defending someone you do not know well is harder. You aren't sure who you can trust. Using a variety of specialized weapons, *karate*, and bravery, a *ninja* may succeed in their quest. The adventures in this book include weapons such as *kusari-fundo, metsubishi* powder, and *shuriken*.

BEWARE and WARNING!

This book is different from other books.

You and YOU ALONE are in charge of what happens in this story.

There are dangers, choices, adventures, and consequences. YOU must use all of your numerous talents and much of your enormous intelligence. The wrong decision could end in disaster—even death. But don't despair. At any time, YOU can go back and make another choice, alter the path of your story, and change its result.

After living and studying in Japan for two years at your friend Nada's *dojo*, you are now living in Oakland, California. You continue to study *ninjutsu* at a local *dojo*, feeling at home and as if you are back in Japan. One day, everything changes when a fellow *aikido* classmate, Saito, runs into you and begins asking you odd questions at the Haiku Tearoom in Japantown. When Saito suddenly gets thrown into a car and all you are left with is a piece of paper with the name of a lounge, you realize you have an important choice to make! Do you utilize your *ninja* training and try to find Saito yourself, OR do you decide to let the police handle it? Good luck!

You throw down your phone in frustration—you still can't get through to Japan. It's the third time you've tried to call your friend Nada, but the call won't go through. She hasn't replied to your emails and hasn't answered her cell phone or your text messages. You thought you might reach her on the landline, but your last resort failed as well.

You're at your family's house in Oakland, California, after living in Japan for almost two years. Originally, you went to study *karate* and Japanese culture. But everything changed very quickly when you met Nada Kurayama. She introduced you to a new discipline called *aikido* at her family *dojo*. It did not take long for the two of you to become fast friends.

Along the way, you discovered a stunning secret about the Kurayama: they are a *ninja* family, going back hundreds of years.

Nada had given up *ninjutsu* for a time because she feared its power. But when her family was threatened by a mysterious sword sent to the *dojo*, she started practicing again. You began to learn the art of the *ninja* as well. Eventually Nada took over the family *dojo*, and you became an instructor. It was an exciting job, but you are relieved in some ways to be back home.

Turn to page 3.

You're now enrolled in a *dojo* in the section of San Francisco known as *Nihonmachi,* or Japantown. This afternoon, as usual, you'd taken the BART train to the *dojo* for *aikido* instruction. You come every day so you don't lose your edge, but it's hard—there are so many distractions back in American life.

After class, you lingered in Japantown, savoring the flavor of the surroundings. You almost felt like you were back in Japan. You went into the Haiku Tearoom for a cup of green tea. You smiled as the tea was prepared in the traditional way, stirred with a bamboo whisk until it foamed.

Your smile dropped when a familiar person entered the tearoom. It was Saito, from your *aikido* class. As he approached, the hairs stood up on the back of your neck. You were sure, that prior to class, you've never met him before. Yet he looked so familiar, it was eerie. Unconsciously, you'd been avoiding him.

Saito sat beside you without asking, without a word of greeting. This did not surprise you. You'd noticed in class that he is very aggressive. He seems to take too much pleasure in putting an opponent on the mat. This is not your style at all. You prefer to think of sparring as a kind of dance where aggression is just one of the steps. You see yourself and your opponent as part of the same flow of energy. "You can turn a hit into a gift," the *sensei,* your master teacher, likes to say. But Saito seems to enjoy aggression for its own sake. He seems to have something to prove.

Turn to the next page.

4

Saito looked on as the tea was served to you. He seemed to feel disdain for the whole ceremony. Maybe he had contempt for the idea that you, an American, would appreciate it. Yet he also seemed to be trying to strike up a conversation with you. He asked how long you'd been practicing *aikido*. You tell him.

"You have pretty good technique," he allowed. When you didn't reply, he went on, "Where did you study before this?"

"In Japan," you answered. "At the Kurayama family *dojo*."

For a moment, Saito's face looked stricken. Then he recovered and continued his questions. You became increasingly uncomfortable, unsure of what he was up to. You mumbled that you had to catch the train back to Oakland and left.

Go on to the next page.

Something about the conversation with Saito haunted you, which was why you finally decided to call Nada. Normally, you keep in touch by email, but you felt the need to talk to her directly.

After you fail to get through and throw your phone, you realize you've been forgetting the sixteen-hour time difference. How ridiculous to forget something so crucial! You're feeling so anxious that you decide to try to stay awake a few hours later than normal in order to call Nada at the time she'd normally be finishing breakfast.

The next thing you know, you look at your watch and realize you've completely overslept! It's time for you to leave for the *dojo*.

During class you feel Saito's eyes on you, but he doesn't say anything. Afterward, you return to the tearoom, looking forward to its warmth and comfort.

You're not surprised when Saito shows up. He appears to have decided you like his company. Your feelings are mixed. There's something intriguing about him, and he's certainly skilled in the martial arts.

On the other hand, you dislike his childish and sometimes abrasive manner. You feel that he's criticizing and trying to impress you at the same time.

Turn to the next page.

6

Though he can't be much more than twenty years old, his face has a worn look, as if he's been through a lot. As he sits down, Saito points to a pair of men drinking tea across the room. "Watch that man lift his cup. See how he's missing part of a finger? He's a *yakuza*—a gangster. They cut off the first joint of their small finger as a sign of loyalty to their boss. It's called *yubitsume*. If they make a mistake, the boss will cut off the rest of the finger."

Turn to page 8.

8

You nod. You know all about the fearful *yakuza* from your stay in Japan.

"Those men are real warriors—not like your friends the Kurayama."

You look up sharply. "What do you know about the Kurayama family?"

"More than I want to know," Saito replies.

"And just how much is that?" you shoot back.

"Too much," he says.

You know this is a game Saito can play forever. Gesturing at the embroidered black jacket he always wears, you say, "I guess you'd rather be with the *yakuza*."

"At least they believe in loyalty and honor," he retorts, getting up abruptly and heading for the door.

You remain seated in the tearoom, baffled. There is a double edge to Saito's words. He seems to want to befriend you, yet when you respond, he turns and attacks you. What does he want?

Go on to the next page.

The screeching sound of tires makes you look up.

A black car has stopped in front of Saito. His face shows panic. Before he can move, two men jump out. One grabs him by the collar of his jacket. They struggle for a moment, tearing the lining. Saito tries to throw the man, but the man knows how to counter the move. He pins Saito's arms behind his back, and the other man delivers a brutal punch to his stomach. Saito doubles over in pain.

You jump from your seat as the men shove him into the car. By the time you're out the door, the car has sped off. Bystanders are staring after it, confused. "Did anyone get the license plate number?" you ask. There is no answer from the baffled crowd.

You look down at the spot where the struggle occurred. A piece of paper has fallen out of Saito's jacket. You stuff it into your pocket and pull out your cell phone to call the police.

Turn to the next page.

At home, you try Nada in Japan again. Your heart sinks when her voicemail picks up. "Nada, I need to talk to you as soon as possible," you say.

You don't have much hope that the police will help. They told you they would investigate, but with so little evidence, they didn't promise much.

You're on your own now, you realize. You unfold the piece of paper that fell out of Saito's jacket. It's a cocktail napkin. The English words across the center translate the Japanese characters at the bottom: SUMIOTO'S KARAOKE LOUNGE.

Go on to the next page.

You turn the napkin over. Handwritten on the other side is the name of a *Pai Gow* club in Oakland, The Black Dragon. *Pai Gow* is a Chinese game played with tiles, resembling a mixture of poker and blackjack. There is also a strange, hand-drawn symbol underneath: inscribed in a diamond are two swords alongside some Japanese characters you can't make out.

You turn the napkin over again, thinking back on Saito's words about the *yakuza*. The men who took him away sure looked like gangsters. The evidence of the karaoke lounge and gambling club add to your suspicion.

Turn to the next page.

12

Is Saito involved with the yakuza? you wonder. And if he is, what should you do about it? You look again at the address on the napkin. Sumioto's is in a dangerous part of the city. Not only that, you know it's a bad idea to cross the *yakuza*. If it turns out Saito is mixed up with them, it's his problem. Why should you put your head on the line for some annoying guy you barely know?

Yet you can't escape the strange sense of familiarity about Saito. You have an inexplicable urge to help him. You're curious about his connection to the Kurayama family. And you wonder if, in his own awkward way, Saito has been asking you for help this past week.

You wish you could talk to Nada, but you can't right now. You're going to have to decide by your-self whether to look into Saito's disappearance or not. Sumioto's would be the logical place to start. But perhaps you should turn the napkin over to the police in the morning and let them handle it.

If you decide to try to help Saito by going to Sumioto's, turn to page 14.

If you decide to let the police handle it, turn to page 48.

With a bloodthirsty scream, you grab Saito from behind and heave both of you off the side of the bridge with a scream of terror.

Then there is silence. You spread your arms in a headfirst fall. You can see nothing but blackness around you. Everything seems to stop—your heart stops, your breathing stops, and yet you are plunging faster and faster toward the water. Hideomi and his men can no longer see you.

Then you slow. You don't feel the bungee cord jerking on your ankles, your fall just goes slower and slower until finally you stop altogether. You reach a bottom point and bounce back up, like a yo-yo on a string. It's the strangest feeling, as if the force of gravity has been powered down, then reversed.

As you bounce up and down at the end of your giant rubber band, you look over to see Saito doing the same thing. He looks at you and starts to laugh uncontrollably. You start laughing, too, so hard it hurts.

Finally the up-and-down boinging stops, and you are suspended in air, halfway between the bridge and the water. You can see the lights of a Coast Guard cutter below. You're glad you made that call. Now you just hope they figure out some way to get you off the bungee cord before all the blood in your body rushes to your head.

The End

14

You can't just abandon Saito to his abductors, you decide. Even though you have misgivings, you head down to the BART station to catch the train into the city. Before you leave, you pack a few *ninja* tools into the hidden inner pockets of your clothing, just in case.

In downtown San Francisco, you decide not to waste time on a bus. You hail a cab and give the address for Sumioto's Karaoke Lounge. The driver looks at you and says, "Are you sure?" You tell him to get going.

As he pulls up in front of the bar, you pay the fare. The driver just shakes his head as he takes your money. You are in a dismal part of town. The sign for Sumioto's blinks on and off, and you head straight for it.

The hostess at the door wears an elegant silk *kimono*. She is young, her lips made up in red. They set in a hard line as soon as she sees you. "Identification, please," she says. "Aren't you a little young for this place?"

You start to explain that you're looking for a friend and just need to ask him a few questions. Her eyes glaze over in incomprehension. You switch to Japanese, but she doesn't want to hear it. "I'll need to see some ID," she repeats, brushing you aside to greet the next set of patrons.

Turn to page 16.

16

Frustrated, you go outside. Maybe there's another way in. Squeezing through a dark alley, you circle around to the back of the building when suddenly you have a strange feeling. You whirl around and face a man who has been following you.

"That door is locked," he says.

You can't make out his face in the dark, but you imagine he has a sinister smile. You go into a defensive mode, ready for anything.

"So, young one, you want to sing in the *karaoke*." *Karaoke* means "empty orchestra." A *karaoke* lounge plays popular music videos while the patrons take turns getting up on stage and singing the songs.

"No," you answer bluntly.

"Ah, but I can tell that you do. Please allow me to escort you. I will see to it that the hostess lets you in."

Turn to page 18.

You follow Saito to Liu's car while Liu gets the rest of the *yakuza* packed off.

"This may come as a shock to you," Saito warns. "But I'm a *ninja* too. In fact—I'm a Kurayama."

You try to act surprised, but you know Saito sees through it. You admit to seeing the Kurayama family seal while you were waiting in his apartment. "Once I knew you were a Kurayama, I figured you also had to be a *ninja*."

Saito asks how you know the family. You tell him about Nada and the time you spent at the family *dojo*. Saito's eyes seem to light up as you talk. "Nada is my best friend in the world," you finish.

"And she's my first cousin!" Saito exclaims. Then he looks sad. "She was one of the ones I couldn't face after I dishonored the family. I worked as a *ninja*-for-hire—a mercenary. I didn't realize how badly the family would look upon it."

Saito pauses, looking out over the bay. "I think I'm ready to return to Japan," he says after a while. "I'll tell the family everything that's happened. They can decide for themselves whether to take me back."

"I'll back you up," you promise. "In fact, this might be just the excuse I need to go back to Japan!"

The End

18

As your eyes adjust to the dim light behind the building, you can see the man's face. It's pockmarked and a deep scar runs across his forehead. He has the look of an outlaw. You can't imagine why he thinks anyone would trust him.

Nevertheless, he seems to be your only ticket into Sumioto's. *Should I accept his invitation?* you wonder. *Or should I give up on trying to get in?* You could go to the *Pai Gow* club, which was also on Saito's napkin. But you might not do any better there.

You pat your sides, reassuring yourself that your *ninja* tools are still there. *I can take care of myself*, you think. Still, this is just the kind of trouble you feared getting into.

If you say yes to the man and allow him to accompany you into the Karaoke Lounge, turn to page 20.

If you refuse his offer, turn to page 81.

20

You take a deep breath. "All right," you say to the man, accepting his invitation to escort you into Sumioto's.

"Excellent," he says, extending a hand. It feels scaly.

You follow him to the front door. He simply nods at the hostess, who lets you through.

"My name is Minoru," he says once you're seated. He's wearing a cheap brown suit with an odd pin on the lapel. "Allow me to buy you a drink."

"Soda with a lime twist," you say quickly. Even though a waitress is coming toward your table, he jumps up to get it from the bar.

While he's gone, you check out the place. It's hot, dirty, and crowded. Most of the patrons are young and tough looking, wearing dark clothes and stylish haircuts. Everyone seems to know each other, but no one is particularly friendly.

You watch as two girls go up on stage to sing a song. The DJ puts on a Japanese pop song. The audience groans.

Go on to the next page.

"Can I get you anything?" You realize the question is directed at you. You look up to see the waitress poised to take your order.

"No," you reply, shaking your head. She gives you an odd look and starts to walk away. You realize her look is one of sympathy.

"Wait—yes!" you say, motioning her back. You cup your hand to the side of your mouth. She leans down to hear. Quietly, in Japanese, you describe Saito and ask if she knows him.

"Oh yes," she whispers back to you. "He works here as a bouncer some nights. But I haven't seen him tonight."

You dig in your pocket and pull out a hefty tip. "Would you mind trying to find out if anyone knows where he is—discreetly?"

With a quick glance to either side, she pockets the tip, nods, and moves on to the next table. You sit back and survey the room, wondering if anyone was watching. Minoru is still at the bar, engaged in conversation.

Turn to the next page.

Your gaze wanders back to the stage, to a slickly dressed pair of guys dancing to a hip-hop song you've heard everywhere since your return. They aren't singing very much, but they're skilled break dancers. They flip and spin, playing off each other's moves. Looking back away from the stage, you see no sign of Minoru or your waitress.

Someone prods you in the ribs. You look behind to see a boy smiling at you and gesturing at the now empty stage. "Your turn," he says.

You freeze, about to shake your head definitely no. Then you feel another prod, and Minoru appears beside you. You wonder if you should have taken your chance to slip away when you had it.

Minoru points to the stage. "Go ahead," he says with a big smile. "Show us your talents."

"I don't want to sing," you tell him.

Minoru tuts reprovingly. "But you must, what's the American saying—you must sing for your dinner?"

Everyone looks at you expectantly. You don't like feeling pressured, but something in you also says, why not?

*If you agree to go up on stage and sing,
turn to page 24.*

*If you decide to shake your head no,
turn to page 96.*

24

For some reason, you realize you don't mind the idea of getting up to sing, in spite of the prodding you've been receiving.

You go to the front of the stage, and the DJ hands you a microphone. "What song?" he asks in Japanese.

"Anything," you say.

He cues up a Japanese pop song from last year. You know it well, though you don't especially like it. The lyrics are displayed on a screen facing you, and a little green ball bounces on top of each word as it's time to sing it. You keep switching your gaze between the screen and the crowd, watching for Saito.

After a few lines, no one pays much attention to you. As you sing, you realize you're in an ideal place to observe the goings-on in the club.

The first thing you notice is that Minoru has an unusual interest in your drink. He's looking at it as if it might explode.

Next you see your waitress coming from the bar with a tray full of drinks. You give her a hard look, asking your question silently. She jerks her head ever so slightly upward and to the back.

You receive polite applause when the song is over. As soon as you rejoin Minoru, he's pushing your drink at you. "A toast," he says with a big, fake smile, "to your singing career."

"Right," you say, raising your glass and pretending to take a sip.

Go on to the next page.

"Listen," you say to Minoru, "can you take me upstairs? I want to see the manager."

Minoru raises his eyebrows. "Sure," he says, after thinking about it. "Finish your drink, and I'll take you up."

"No," you say firmly, "I want to go now."

Minoru gives you a strange look, but shrugs. "Okay, we'll go now."

You follow him as he winds his way through the club, moving a bit slowly and saying hello to everyone. Your waitress gives you a worried look as you pass her.

You nearly bump into Minoru as he stops to fumble with a door at the back of the bar. This gives you a chance to get a closer look at the pin on his lapel. You recognize it—it's the same design drawn on Saito's cocktail napkin. Now you know you're on the scent.

Minoru gets the door open and leads you up a flight of creaky wooden stairs. As you reach the top, you tap him on the back as if to ask a question. The moment he turns, you cloud his vision with a spell of invisibility.

Now you're in *ninja* mode. You move silently down the narrow hallway, stopping to listen at each door. You hear nothing. Another flight of stairs lies at the end of the hall, but you hesitate in the hallway.

Turn to the next page.

You go back down the hallway and put your ear to one of the doors. No sounds come, yet you sense something is happening inside. Then you hear it—a moan.

Suddenly, from the other side of the door, a male voice shouts, "Come on, Saito, you coward. Do it!"

Moving with stealth, you try the doorknob. It turns. You crack open the door without a sound and peer in.

The scene inside is appalling. All five men in the room have their eyes locked on Saito, who is seated at a center table. In one hand he holds a small silver knife, the little finger of the other poised underneath. He is about to undergo the *yakuza* initiation of *yubitsume*—ritual finger cutting.

You must act now and stop this. You close the door and pull tools from your pockets: firecrackers, a smoke bomb, *metsubishi*, and *shuriken*. Then you tie a bandana over your mouth as a mask. Lighting the fuse on the smoke bomb, you place it in front of the door. Then you light the firecrackers and throw them down the hall. As their fuses burn down, you wedge yourself crosswise between the walls of the corridor and, alternating between your feet and hands for leverage, inch your way upward to avoid the explosion and stay out of sight.

You're almost at ceiling height when the fuses burn to the end. Everything goes off at once. The firecrackers sound like rifles and smoke billows through the hallway.

Go on to the next page.

Two men burst out the door, choking on the smoke. "Check the stairs!" orders the voice you heard before. The men curse and cough as they run down the hall to the stairway.

The next two come out of the door together. You fling the *metsubishi* in their eyes, then drop from the ceiling and land on their shoulders. Straddling their heads between your knees, you scissor your legs together, knocking them out. The three of you crash to the floor.

Disentangling yourself from the men, you get to your feet and rush into the room, your *shuriken* ready. You freeze, finding yourself face-to-face with the last man—the boss. He holds a gun in his hand and looks as if he's going to get a lot of pleasure out of pulling the trigger.

Turn to the next page.

28

Suddenly there is a thunk on his neck, and the boss crumples to the ground. Saito emerges from behind him. "You!" he cries with shock.

Before you can answer, you feel intense heat at your back. Flames are leaping through the doorway—your smoke bomb must have ignited the old, dry wood of the building!

"We've got to get out of here!" you cry to Saito. "This place is a tinderbox!"

"The window!" Saito says, grabbing your arm.

But you resist. You're on the second floor. With your *ninja* skills, you know you can survive the jump, but what about Saito? Maybe you'd be better off trying to get out with the crowd in the confusion downstairs.

If you decide to go to the window with Saito, turn to page 30.

If you tell Saito to come down the stairs, turn to page 67.

The room fills with smoke. You slide open the window and gulp in breaths of fresh air. You can make out the flat roof of a garage below you. At least, you hope that's what it is. There's no time to be choosy. You climb through the window and leap into the dark.

You make a head-over-heels flip, landing with several rolls on the tar roof of the garage. Getting to your feet, you see Saito about to try the same thing.

"No!" you cry, but he's already in the air. To your surprise, he executes the jump perfectly.

As Saito brushes himself off, you start to say, "Where did you learn—"

"Later," he cuts you off.

"Right," you agree. You find a place to climb down off the garage and escape down a dark alley. Fire sirens scream in the distance.

You keep running for several blocks until you're sure no one has followed you. Finally you stop, panting for breath. You and Saito look at one another. His face breaks into a smile. Holding up a pinkie, he says, "I'm grateful, right down to the tips of my fingers."

"That was a *yakuza* initiation ceremony, right? But why would you—"

"It's a long story," Saito interrupts, sighing. "Don't worry, you'll get to hear it. Let's get someplace safe first—back to my apartment?"

"You call that safe?" you reply. "The *yakuza* probably already have it staked out. No, we'd better go back to my house."

Turn to page 32.

32

You reach the BART station just in time to catch the last train to Oakland for the night. Once home, with the doors and windows locked, you relax. You make a pot of tea for Saito and yourself. Without any prompting, he starts telling you his story.

Born into a respected family with a long *bujutsu* tradition, from an early age Saito excelled at the martial arts. Before long, he was groomed to take over the family *dojo*.

"But two years ago, I made a mistake," he says. "I took money for my skills. I figured, why live like a monk? I just wanted a few of the good things in life. My family didn't appreciate it at all. They said I was a mercenary, a soldier for hire. I had disgraced their name.

"I was fed up with tradition. I left Japan to make a new start in this country. It was easy to find work teaching *karate*, but it wasn't enough. I got bored. I guess I lost my way. I started hanging out with what you might call the wrong sort of people— staying out late, shooting pool, and that kind of stuff. My downfall, though, was getting hooked on *Pai Gow*."

"At The Black Dragon," you put in.

Go on to the next page.

Saito nods with a little surprise, then goes on, "Right. At first I did very well. I could sense what was going to happen. But the late nights took a toll on me and I lost my touch. I began to lose. But the more I lost, the more I played, trying to win it back. Needless to say, I lost even more. I owed way more than I could pay. So I borrowed from the only place I could—from the *yakuza*."

Turn to the next page.

34

"When I missed my first payment," Saito continues, "the *yakuza* gave me a good working over. My *karate* was useless against them. Besides, I'd gotten rusty. They told me I'd have to start working for them as a bouncer at the *karaoke* lounge. And that was just to keep up with their interest payments.

"I decided to reform. I visited a famous *sensei* who had retired to the Marin hills, Arthur Wujan. He told me to start practicing *aikido* again and come back when I'd paid off my debt. I worked as a dishwasher in a coffee shop until three, I took classes at the *dojo*, then worked as a bouncer at Sumioto's, all in one day. But I lost patience. I decided to try a shortcut with *Pai Gow* again. Only this time, I wouldn't wait for luck to come. I'd cheat.

"Unfortunately, I was caught. The *oya-bun*, Hideomi, the *yakuza* boss, was enraged, to say the least. He said the only way I could atone was to do more of his dirty work. My first job was to go down to the waterfront with some other thugs and break up a dockworkers' strike. I did it—I beat up the union guys—but I felt terrible. That night I vowed I'd never work for the *yakuza* again.

"When I didn't report in to Hideomi yesterday, his men came looking for me. Up there, above Sumioto's, he said there was only one way to ensure my loyalty. I had to become one of them. I would have to go through the initiation—the *yubitsume*. Then, if I ever betrayed them, they would have the right to kill me."

Turn to page 36.

"Luckily," Saito finishes, "you showed up just in time. I was seconds away from becoming a *yakuza*."

"The bad news is, they probably still want to kill you—and now me as well," you comment. "Not only did we burn down the building, we don't know if Hideomi survived."

Saito shrugs. Right now all I care about is that I have a reprieve. I just wish I knew what to do next."

"So do I," you say. You pause, giving Saito a penetrating look. He refuses to meet your eyes. "You're not telling me everything. Tonight, when we jumped from the window, I saw something— where did you learn the art of the *ninja*?"

Saito hangs his head. "I might as well tell you," he murmurs. "You see, I was not so surprised to discover that you knew *ninjutsu*. After all, anyone who studied with the Kurayama…"

His voice trails off. You have to lean forward to hear what he says next. "You see, I, too, am a Kurayama. Your friend Nada is my first cousin."

You let out a long, slow breath. It all begins to make sense. Except for one thing.

"I don't understand," you say. "When you got into trouble, why didn't you go back? They're a forgiving family. I know they'd take you—"

Saito holds up his hand to stop you. "Yes. They might take me back. But it is my choice. It is my pride. I will return when I am ready."

You want to argue, but you are tired. "Let's sleep on it," you say. "We can decide what to do in the morning."

Go on to the next page.

The next morning you wake up to the sun shining through your window. But the nice feeling of sunshine quickly disappears when you remember what happened the day before.

The news gets worse when you read through the local news from the night before. There is a story about the fire at Sumioto's. No one was killed, but a police detective is quoted as saying that two people are wanted for arson. Their description fits you and Saito!

Saito walks into the kitchen, yawning. You tell him the bad news. He yawns again. "It's not the police I'm worried about," he says.

"Then let's turn ourselves in," you say. "We can give them evidence about Hideomi's gang and clear ourselves of the arson charge at the same time."

Saito looks at you as if you're crazy. "If we go to the police, Hideomi will know exactly where we are. Maybe we'd only spend a few nights in jail, but that'd be long enough. You don't think there are *yakuza* on the inside?"

"Suppose you tell me what you propose to do then," you snap. Saito seems to be recovering from his gratitude and returning to his former self.

"I propose to die," Saito replies. You don't react, so he explains, "Not literally. But I'll stage my death for Hideomi's benefit. Then at least he won't be tracking me down. I'll have a chance to escape."

Turn to the next page.

You have another idea. "Let's go to Japan, Saito. If we can get to the Kurayama *dojo*, I know they can protect us."

"No way," Saito answers. "I told you already, I'm not ready to go back yet."

You're exasperated. You can see he's not going to budge on going to Japan. But should you go along with his plan to stage his own death?

If you decide to help Saito fake his own death, turn to page 41.

If you try to convince him to leave the country instead, turn to page 84.

"Go ahead and shoot," the captain snarls, advancing on you. Debbie takes a breath and pulls the trigger. The gun jams. Iwata runs up and grabs it from her. "Everyone back down below!" he commands, herding the three of you to your prison.

Turn to the next page.

40

The captain keeps his gun trained on you while Iwata unties the smuggler you caught. Two more crew members arrive.

"Bring some chains," Iwata orders. He turns to you. "Minoru was right. There's always one bad apple in the bunch. And there's only one thing you can do with it—toss it out."

As the crew wraps you up in chains, you realize that Iwata is not using a figure of speech.

The End

"How will we convince Hideomi you died?" you ask.

Saito outlines his plan to you. You'll make it look like you both jump off the Golden Gate Bridge. But bungee cords will be attached to your ankles to prevent you from hitting the water.

You stare at him and say quietly, "You're insane."

"I know," he replies. "But it's the only thing that's going to save my life."

"Do you really expect me to trust this 'bungee cord' thing to catch me?"

"Believe me, they work. People jump from great heights with them all the time."

Without waiting for your accord, he picks up the telephone and dials. You can understand most of what he's saying in Japanese. Fear fills his face, and you know he's talking to Hideomi.

"I am ready to become a *yakuza*," he says. "For real this time."

Saito listens while Hideomi says something to him.

"Yes," Saito says, "Here with me, tied up." Then you know who they're talking about—you! "Okay, we will both come. The Golden Gate Bridge—midnight."

Saito hangs up. He looks at you triumphantly.

"He said he didn't believe me, but I know it's going to work. He's so devoted to the *yakuza*, he says he knows I will join them."

Turn to the next page.

Saito goes off to find a pair of bungee cords and the other supplies he needs to make his plan work. You take your cell phone into a quiet corner of the house and make a few calls of your own. It never hurts to have a backup plan, like the police.

Fifteen minutes before midnight, you and Saito stand waiting for Hideomi on the Golden Gate Bridge. Everything is set. You both wear baggy pants. Underneath them are bungee cords, secured to your ankles. The other end of the cords are tied to the base of the bridge railing.

You aren't sure you really want to go through with this. Luckily it's dark, and you can't see the water below.

The walkway on the bridge is lit, though, and you spot Hideomi and his men in the distance. They're wearing black suits with thin white ties and white shoes, just like in the movies. They haven't spotted you yet.

Saito makes sure the rope around your wrists appears to be bound tightly. He grabs hold of a cable and climbs up on the railing of the bridge. Then he helps you up beside him. You balance precariously on the edge of the abyss, leaning against a cable with your shoulder. It's unnerving to be without the use of your hands. The wind swirls below you.

Turn to the next page.

44

Finally, Hideomi sees you. When he's within ten feet, Saito holds up his hand, halting the approaching *yakuza*. He pulls a short sword from the ceremonial robe he is wearing over his clothes. It is the kind used for *seppuku*, or ritual suicide.

Pushing the sword out from his chest with both hands, Saito cries, "Hideomi, I dedicate my life to you!"

"Wait!" one of Hideomi's men cries. "Check the sword."

Saito hesitates, the sword in the air. Form must be followed. Hideomi nods to his man, who comes forward to inspect the sword. If he does so, he'll see that it's a fake—it has a spring-operated retractable point.

The only way the fake suicide can proceed is if you pretend to attack Saito from behind, toppling the two of you over the edge. If you're lucky, Hideomi will believe you've plunged into the bay to your death.

On the other hand, you're not at all sure you want to make the bungee dive. Your backups should arrive soon. Maybe it's time for a change of plan.

If you pretend to attack Saito, turn to page 13.

If you let the man take the sword from Saito, go on to the next page.

You keep still, concentrating on your balance while Hideomi's man approaches Saito. Saito starts to hand over the sword. The man grabs his wrist and pulls him down off the railing. You jump down after him.

As the *yakuza* inspects the sword, you hear two cars screech to a stop on the bridge. Plainclothes officers pile out, ordering everyone to freeze. Guns appear in everyone's hands.

As the officers approach, everyone starts screaming at once. The *yakuza* with the sword yells at Saito for betraying them. He plunges the sword into Saito's chest, but it simply retracts into itself. Hideomi demands the detective in charge arrest you and Saito immediately because you're the arsonists who set fire to the Karaoke Lounge. You try to tell the officer that you're guilty of nothing, and Hideomi is a *yakuza*.

"Shut up!" the detective shouts. "You can all do your talking down at the station." He has his men disarm and handcuff all of you. The *yakuza* are bundled into one car, and you and Saito into another.

Doors slam, and the detective gets into the passenger side of your car. "Let's go," he orders the driver. The driver turns on the siren and peels out.

Turn to the next page.

46

A little way across the bridge something suddenly jerks on your leg. You and Saito are thrust against the door as if some incredible force were trying to pull you out of the car. The pull on your leg increases, and you scream in pain.

The same invisible force seems to take control of the wheel, jerking the car to the right, causing it to bounce against the curb a few times before the driver jams on the brakes. As soon as he does, the car is dragged backward several feet, slightly relieving the stress on your leg.

"The bungee cords!" you cry. "We forgot to take them off."

"I told you they were strong," Saito says, grimacing as he tries to release his ankle.

"What the devil!?" the detective exclaims, glaring back at you.

"Put the car in reverse," Saito tells the driver.

Go on to the next page.

Once you've gotten yourselves untied from the bungee cords, Saito explains his plan to the officers. "What a couple of idiots!" the detective explodes. "At the very best, you're going to be charged with malicious mischief and destroying police property—if we don't get you for arson."

A few minutes later, the detective looks back at you and Saito and says in a quiet voice, "You'd better have the goods on Hideomi."

As it turns out, Saito does. He produces enough evidence to put Hideomi and his men away. All charges against you are dismissed. You're both put in the witness protection program to keep you safe from the *yakuza*. One of these days, the welt on your ankle will heal. And another one of these days, you'll go back to Japan with Saito to help him reconcile with Nada and his family. But for now, you're just glad you didn't have to make that jump.

The End

48

You're not going to stick your neck out for Saito. The situation is too dangerous, and you have too few clues. As you get ready for bed, you try to just forget about him.

You wake up in the morning and go about your business, but the image of Saito being punched yesterday keeps coming back. You know how skilled he is in self-defense. Anyone who could do that to him can't be good.

Soon it's time to take the train into San Francisco. On your way to the *dojo*, you stop by the police station to drop off the cocktail napkin. No one there seems very interested in the piece of evidence you have. They tell you that most of the time a missing person case solves itself. You reply that Saito's not missing, he's kidnapped.

At the *dojo*, you tell your fellow students what happened yesterday. They're surprised; no one has any idea what it could be about, but they don't seem very interested in trying to find out. No one knows, or likes, Saito very well. They advise you not to worry, it will sort itself out.

You try to put the whole thing out of your mind. But you don't feel good about it.

Go on to the next page.

Two days later, walking down a sidewalk in Japantown, you're startled to see Saito approaching you. Your paths cross at a bus stop. He stops and greets you but then looks away. His face is puffy.

"What happened?" you ask bluntly. "Where have you been?"

"I've got a job. I haven't been able to come to class."

"I mean with those men who took you away."

He dismisses it with a wave of his left hand. There's something strange about him. After a moment, you realize what it is. Saito is keeping his right hand stuffed in his pocket.

A bus approaches. Saito automatically pulls his hand from his pocket for the fare. That's when you see that he's missing the top joint of his little finger. Even under the bandage, you can tell the finger is shorter than the others.

"Saito!" you gasp. "What happened to your finger?"

"Mind your own business," he snaps, stepping up to the bus. You grab the back of his jacket.

"Saito, is it a *yakuza*—"

You stop in midsentence, suddenly aware that people are staring at you.

"Let me go," Saito says angrily, pulling away.

Conflicting thoughts flash through your mind. You're tempted to do as Saito asks—to let him go, and just be done with him. Yet a small voice inside tells you that if you do, you'll never see him again, and that he needs your help.

If you let Saito go, turn to the next page.

If you insist on talking to him, turn to page 52.

50

You let go of Saito's jacket and step away from the bus. "Call me," you say to his back. He doesn't turn around. "If you need help," you add. You're not sure if he heard you. The rest of the passengers file on to the bus. The doors whoosh shut.

Walking over to the tearoom, you feel strangely depressed. You order tea and a sweet cake, but they don't taste right. You leave the cake half-eaten and wander around Japantown. A cold fog blows in from the ocean. Darkness begins to fall, and the lights in the city come on one by one.

Every day for the next week, you stop at the tearoom after class. You stay as long as you can, reading the newspaper, hoping Saito will show up.

But there is no sign of him—that is until you see his picture in the newspaper. Your heart sinks like a stone. As you read the story, it's as if you already know what it will say. Police found his body floating in the bay. They believe his death is tied to crime syndicate activity and that he may be the same man who was reported kidnapped in Japantown ten days earlier.

For reasons you can't explain, you feel terribly bad about the death of this man you barely knew. You'll never escape the feeling you could have helped him.

The End

You tug hard on Saito's jacket, pulling him off the first step of the bus. He turns as if to hit you, but you look him directly in the eyes. He lowers his arm.

"Let's have a cup of tea," you say, leading him away from the bus. He brushes your hand away but walks along with you.

You find a table and order. Saito heaves a big sigh, then stares off out the window. You're not sure what to say. "So what's your new job?" you venture.

It takes him a while to answer. "Oh, it's just..." he trails off, still staring out the window.

Suddenly, Saito looks directly at you. "Stealing guns," he blurts.

"Where, um, where do you steal them from?"

Saito bursts into laughter. "The art of polite conversation," he comments. "The question is not where, but why."

"I was getting to that," you say. Saito looks down into his tea. You can't help staring at his bandaged finger. "Who were those men who took you away?" you ask quietly.

"You've already figured it out—they're *yakuza*," he admits.

"But why did they attack you like that?"

He sips his tea. "Because I owe them money."

Go on to the next page.

Saito pauses, watching you. "I made some bad decisions, got in over my head," he explains. "I had to borrow money from the *yakuza*. Now it's time to pay them back. They're collecting the only way they can.

"You see," Saito goes on, "the *yakuza* have a problem. In Japan, guns are strictly controlled. But these days, the *yakuza* feel they need them to conduct business. The demand for guns in Japan is very high. The United States, meanwhile, has an abundant supply. Simple economics says hook up the demand with the supply.

"Of course," Saito continues, "they prefer not to pay for the guns. So they steal them. Then, when they have a shipment ready, they smuggle them over to Japan. But first, they need someone to take the shipment down to the docks—and, if caught, to take the rap. That's where I come in. The *yakuza* think it's the least I can do to help work off some of my debt. That's why they picked me up the other day—to give me my assignment."

"Tell them you can't do it," you cut in. "Tell them you'll pay them back another way."

He smirks, as if at some private joke. "If I say no to the *yakuza*, I'm a dead man."

You place your hands around your cup and think about the taste of the tea. You're stumped.

"I'm starved," Saito declares, putting both hands on the table. "Let's go get some dinner."

"Sushi?" you suggest.

"I hate sushi," he says. "Let's get a hamburger."

Turn to the next page.

54

You go outside with Saito to his motor scooter. "Wait a minute," you say. "I thought you were taking the bus."

Saito grins. "Just trying to avoid you."

You shake your head and smile, then hop on the back of the scooter. Saito loans you his helmet for the ride over to The Happy Boy, his favorite diner.

As you eat, Saito tells you his story—at least most of it. You have a feeling he's leaving something out.

Saito grew up in Japan, he tells you, where his family ran a *karate dojo*. He was an excellent student and advanced very quickly. From an early age, he was in line to become the *sensei* of the *dojo*. But something happened. Trying to make money outside the *dojo*, he fell into disgrace and dishonored his family. Fed up with Japanese tradition, he came to the United States to start over.

But somewhere along the way, he lost his original purpose. He had no problem finding work teaching *karate*, but before long he got bored. He started staying out late at nightclubs and gambling dens. He got hooked on *Pai Gow*, a Chinese game similar to poker and blackjack.

With his keen sense of perception, he was able to win money at *Pai Gow*. But as he left behind his martial arts discipline and lived the fast life, he lost his touch. He began to lose. He played more, only to lose more.

Turn to page 56.

Finally, Saito was forced to borrow money from the only place he could get it—the *yakuza*. When he failed to make his first loan payment, the *oya-bun,* or *yakuza* boss, put him to work as a bouncer at Sumioto's Karaoke Lounge.

Saito knew that he'd be in trouble if he got too involved with the *yakuza*, so he vowed to reform. He visited a reclusive *sensei* named Arthur Wujan in the hills of Marin and told him he wanted to become his disciple. Wujan told him to return when he had worked off his debt.

Saito went to work eighteen hours a day: he washed dishes in a restaurant, began practicing *aikido*, and worked at the bar at night. But he decided he needed a shortcut. He went back to the *Pai Gow* club. This time he was sure he could win—he would cheat.

The only hitch was he got caught. Hideomi, the *yakuza oya-bun*, was furious. He forced Saito to take on rougher jobs for the gang. He was sent down to the waterfront with some other thugs to break up a dockworkers' strike. They succeeded, but after that night, Saito vowed never to work for the *yakuza* again.

"They changed my mind pretty fast, though," Saito says. "You saw their method of inviting me over for a chat. Hideomi decided it was time for me to become one of them. He forced me to go through the initiation, which included cutting off the tip of my finger in order to prove my loyalty. He also gave me my first job, which is this gun-smuggling run. It's set for tomorrow night."

Go on to the next page.

"But can't you pay them back? Why don't you sell your scooter? Or—I'll help you," you volunteer.

Saito laughs. "My scooter wouldn't even cover the first payment. Besides, it's too late," he says, holding up his finger.

"I can't go back. Once you've been initiated, you're bound for life. It's called *gin*, or obligation."

"But you didn't really mean it when you got initiated, did you?"

Saito shrugs. "That doesn't matter. In their eyes, if I betray them, they have the right to kill me."

Turn to the next page.

58

"So you're just going to go along with this?" you ask.

"No," Saito says quietly. "I'm going to nail these guys somehow."

"Can't you just go somewhere else?"

Saito shakes his head. "They'd find me. The only way I could escape this is if I could escape my skin. Now there's an idea—plastic surgery." He bursts out laughing.

"What's so funny?" you say.

"Where would I get the money for plastic surgery?" he says, still laughing.

Suddenly you realize how serious he is. Saito notices the look on your face and says, "It's stupid to be telling you all this. What can you do? You're just a kid."

Go on to the next page.

"I'll do whatever I can," you hear yourself say.

"I don't want you mixed up in this," he replies firmly. This is a side of Saito you haven't seen—concern for another. "It may not happen tomorrow night, but sooner or later I'll help nab these guys. My days will be numbered when I do, but I'd rather die that way than spend my life as a *yakuza*."

There must be another way, you think. Desperately you try to come up with a plan. You see an image of Nada's *dojo* in Japan. Surely Saito would be safe there, if only you could convince him to go with you.

But he seems determined to live out his fate. Maybe you should try to come up with a plan to trap the *yakuza*. At least that would buy you both some time—an extra day at the very least.

If you try to convince Saito to leave town, turn to the next page.

If you try to come up with a plan to trap the yakuza, turn to page 68.

"Saito, you've got to get out of town," you say. "I know we can find a place for you to hide. I have friends in Japan who can protect you."

Saito shakes his head slowly. "If you mean the Kurayama, forget it."

"What about Arthur Wujan, then? Won't he help you now?"

"I'm not running away," Saito says firmly.

"Quit trying to be a hero!" you say in exasperation.

"I'm no hero!" he explodes. "I'm just a jerk who's got himself in a lot of trouble, and now for once in my life, I'm going to face the consequences of my actions!"

"You don't have to die for making a few mistakes," you say softly.

Saito crumples up his napkin and throws it on the table. "It's time to go," he says, not looking at you.

Silently you pay the bill and walk out of The Happy Boy. "I'll give you a ride to the train station," Saito says.

"Nevermind," you say. "I'll walk."

You're fuming as you head to the BART station. You decide that you're done with trying to help Saito. He's hopeless.

Turn to page 62.

But that night at home, you can't sleep. You toss and turn in bed, trying to think of a way to get Saito out of his predicament. *He's being too hard on himself,* you think. *He seems determined to punish himself for his mistakes.*

There's one last straw you can grasp. Arthur Wujan is a legendary *sensei*. You doubt he'd take the time to help you, but he did tell Saito he might take him on as a student. If you can get Saito to visit him again, maybe he can help find a way out.

You wake up at six. You find Saito's number from your class's contact list. He answers the phone almost immediately. "Are you awake?" you ask.

"Yes," he says. "I didn't sleep too well."

Sensing that Saito's mood has changed, you waste no time. You propose your idea of going to see Arthur Wujan for advice right away. Saito agrees it's a good idea. "I'll pick you up at the BART station on my scooter," he says.

You quickly dress. An hour later, you're on the back of Saito's scooter crossing the Golden Gate Bridge. Fog swirls through the towers. Every once in a while, you get a glimpse of the waves crashing below.

Once you're in Marin County, Saito takes a narrow, winding road that climbs higher and higher into the hills. He turns off onto a tiny dirt road and bumps down to a modest wood house set in a clump of live oaks. Saito points to an addition on the house that's as large as the original. "That's the *dojo*," he says.

Turn to page 64.

64

Arthur Wujan is waiting at the door for you. He's a small, bent man with long stray wisps of hair on his head and face. His pants are baggy, and his shirt hangs loose on his shoulders. His greeting is gruff, but he quickly offers you a cup of tea as he leads you to a small room next to the kitchen.

You sit cross-legged at a low table. He prepares the tea silently, and you sip it for a few minutes without saying anything. Finally Wujan asks Saito how his project is going.

"Not so well, *sensei*," Saito says. He looks down, then launches into the whole story of what has happened since Wujan last saw him. "We have come to seek your advice," Saito finishes humbly.

Wujan turns to you. He clears his throat. "Obviously, you care about this boy whom you hardly know. Tell me honestly: is he ready to start again?"

Turn to page 66.

You relate some of your conversation from the night before. "Saito was willing to give up his life," you say.

A little smile plays across Wujan's lips. "The moment you have given up is the moment you are ready to begin," he says. "Saito, if you like, you may stay here. You will be safe from the *yakuza*. You will be my student."

Saito bows his head. "I am honored, *sensei*. I would like to stay."

"Good," Wujan says. He shuffles over to a corner and brings Saito a broom. "You can start by sweeping out the *dojo*."

As Saito leaves the room, Wujan shares a complicit smile.

"Keep him on his toes," you say.

Wujan gives you a ride down to a bus station. You're glad Saito's safe. However, you never did figure out what was so familiar-looking about him.

The End

"We can't jump!" you cry to Saito. "Let's take the stairs."

Without giving him a chance to answer, you pull Saito out of the door. Blinded by the smoke, he stumbles over the inert bodies in the hallway. You help him up, but the smoke from the fire starts to overcome you.

You run smack into the first two men who came out the door. You can't believe they've come back up the stairs—until the word *girt* flashes through your mind: loyalty. The men must have come back for their boss and comrades. It doesn't occur to you that perhaps they've come back for revenge.

You try to slip by them, thinking they want only to get back to the room. But one of them pistol-whips you on the back of the head, and the other knocks out Saito.

You're only half-conscious as they drag you down the hall and throw you into a closet. Vaguely, somewhere in the back of your mind, you hear the door being locked. In this room, there are no windows. But you're lucky in one respect—by the time the flames reach you, the smoke has made you unconscious.

The End

68

"Let's not waste any time—let's try to trap the *yakuza* tomorrow night," you say to Saito. "I'll help you."

"No way," Saito responds. "You're not getting mixed up in this."

"Listen, Saito, you can't do it alone. You at least need a backup. Besides, I've got a plan."

Saito regards you skeptically. "What's your plan?"

You think furiously. "Will Hideomi be with you?"

"Yes," Saito says, "I guess he wants to watch my work firsthand."

"So what's the deal? Where do you pick up the shipment?"

"The guns are waiting in a garage on Geary Street. I'm supposed to meet Hideomi at his headquarters. We'll go to the garage, load up the guns, and take them down to the docks. A trawler waiting offshore will signal when they're ready to take on cargo."

"Okay, here's what we'll do," you say, and proceed to outline your plan.

Go on to the next page.

Saito reluctantly agrees that the plan just might work. You don't mention to him that you're also going to try to bring some help.

You go home and call your friends Kurt and Keiku from the *dojo*. They agree to help you out. Then, before you go to bed, you open a bag you brought back from Japan. It contains all the *ninja* tools you'll need for tomorrow night.

You meet Kurt and Keiku at the *dojo* the next afternoon. Kurt has a car, and you arrange to have them pick you up in three hours. After class, you walk a few blocks down to the police station. You have an appointment with Detective Liu, the officer who is investigating Saito's disappearance.

After setting things up with Detective Liu, you walk a few blocks more to Saito's apartment. He buzzes you in the front door, and you climb a dark stairway to the third floor. The apartment is small, little more than a room with a bed and a utility kitchen.

Turn to page 71.

As Saito brews you a cup of tea on a hot plate, you notice he looks worried. When you ask him why, he explains, "It's been a long time since I've done anything like this. Anything that might require fighting, that is. I'm not sure I'm up to it."

It's unlike Saito to express such doubts. Suddenly, you realize that must have been why he was so aggressive in class—to make up for his insecurities. "Don't worry," you tell him. "I just talked to Detective Liu. He'll be there. We won't have to do any fighting."

You go over the plan one more time with Saito. You're not really sure that you can avoid all fighting, but your words help him relax. Saito glances at his watch. "It's time for me to go. Wish me luck—wish us luck."

You have an hour before Kurt and Keiku show up. Your gaze wanders up and down Saito's desk. Something in a half-opened drawer catches your eye. You pull out a yellowed piece of parchment. At the top of the page is the crest of the Kurayama family, your hosts when you lived in Japan.

You glance over the parchment, your heart pounding. Although you can speak Japanese fairly well, your reading is limited. But you can make out enough to realize one thing: Saito is a Kurayama. Suddenly it seems as if a lot more is at stake tonight than catching some *yakuza*.

Turn to the next page.

Before you know it, the door buzzer sounds. You grab your bag, lock the door behind you, and run down the stairs. Kurt has the car running. "Do you have your camera?" you ask Keiku. She nods.

Kurt drives carefully over the hills of San Francisco. You've got plenty of time. You cross Market Street and roll down the wide avenues of the warehouse district. After you cross the railroad tracks, the dark waters of the bay are in front of you.

You tell Kurt where to park. Hoisting your bag over your shoulder, you lead your two friends through dim alleys toward the waterfront. The pungent smell of the bay grows stronger.

Go on to the next page.

Soon you hear the sound of lapping water. You go along the dockside until you find the warehouse number you want. An iron fire escape climbs its back. You pull a *kaginawa* from your bag, swing it in a loop, and toss it up toward the fire ladder. It hooks on the bottom rung, and you climb the rope. Gesturing to Kurt and Keiku to wait, you silently ascend the iron stairway to the roof of the warehouse.

As you begin to pull yourself over the lip, your sharp eyes pick up some movement. You drop back down just enough to peer over the edge. Two bulky figures are on the roof—and they're heading in your direction.

Turn to the next page.

You move back down from the edge of the roof and press yourself into the shadows against the wall. Voices whisper urgently to one another in Japanese. You stay completely still as they look over the spot you just occupied. Then they move away.

Cautiously you pull yourself back up over the lip. In the rooftop moonlight, you can see the two men. Their hair is short, and they are wearing sleeveless t-shirts, yet their shoulders seem swathed in color tattoos. The men must be *yakuza!*

What are they doing here? Are they backups for the job? Or do they have some other purpose—like trying to hijack the gun shipment?

You are startled to hear Kurt whisper from below, "Can we come up yet?" You almost shush him, but you hold your breath. The footsteps of the two men quickly approach the roof edge. Your friends have been discovered.

What now? You can try to escape, or you can take on the two *yakuza* yourself. Your decision depends partly on why you think the men are here. If they are Hideomi's men, you don't want to have anything to do with them. But if they're not, maybe you can convince them to team up with you.

One of the men shines a flashlight toward Kurt and Keiku. He still doesn't know you're there. You have about three seconds to decide what to do.

---

*If you decide to confront the men,
go on to the next page.*

If you decide to keep silent, turn to page 76.

You pull yourself back up to the roof, surprising the two *yakuza*. One of them immediately has a gun trained on you.

"Don't worry," you say, raising your hands. "We're on the same side. We both want to get Hideomi, right?"

Your words take a moment to register. Then the men laugh. "Right, we want to get Hideomi," one says. "We want to get him little weasels like you and Saito. Now, tell your friends down there to come up."

In a flash you realize you've made a terrible mistake. These are Hideomi's men. This whole thing is a setup—a test of Saito's loyalty. And you've just given him away.

You have one last hope. "It's a trap!" you call down to Keiku and Kurt. "Run!"

Something smashes down on the side of your head. Suddenly everything goes black.

When you regain consciousness, you feel as if you are swinging in a hammock. But you're terribly heavy. It is then that you realize you are wrapped in heavy chains. The *yakuza* are swinging you back and forth, about to heave you into the bay!

You wonder if Keiku and Kurt will be able to save Saito; they're definitely too late to save you. As you go sailing through the air, you know you'll have a hard time swimming in this outfit.

The End

76

You keep perfectly still as the two *yakuza* peer down from the roof. They still haven't seen you. One of them clambers onto the fire escape. You grab his leg, twist it, and flip him onto the metal landing below. He's out cold.

You swing over to the other side and pull yourself up to the roof just as something hard and metal clangs against the spot on the wall you just vacated. The moment you land on the roof, you crouch and roll to your left. The other *yakuza* turns and swings at you with a metal club, just missing you. You spring to your feet. The *yakuza* comes at you again, but you keep twisting and dodging backward, avoiding his strikes.

Something tells you you're nearing the edge of the warehouse. Instinctively, you know your next move. As the man lunges at you again, you pitch yourself forward, cutting him down at his feet. Surprised, he can't stop his momentum. He goes flying over you and the edge of the building. A second later you hear a big splash.

Running back to the fire escape, you hear Kurt's voice. "What's going on?" he cries.

"A couple of Hideomi's men were waiting for us up here," you explain breathlessly. "I'll take care of the one on the fire escape. You two go fish the other one out of the water and tie him up."

You have plenty of rope in your bag. The man on the fire escape is still unconscious. You bind him securely to the grillwork. By the time you're done, Keiku and Kurt have brought over the other man, bound and gagged and dripping wet.

Go on to the next page.

"Saito and Hideomi will arrive any minute," you say to Keiku and Kurt. "Climb up the fire escape and back us up if we have any trouble."

Your two friends nod, and you race off to the other side of the building. The van comes squealing around the corner just as you hide in a doorway. Hideomi gets out of the passenger door, all business. Saito gets out more slowly.

Hideomi strides to the dock edge and peers across the water. "Look for the trawler," he instructs Saito. "It should be here soon."

"I doubt there is any trawler," you say, emerging from the darkened doorway. You hold a ten-foot *kusari-fundo*, or *ninja* chain, across the palms of your hands.

Hideomi just turns and smiles, as if he's been expecting you. He whistles up to the warehouse roof.

"Your men aren't there any more," you inform him. Kurt and Keiku appear at the edge.

Without a word, Hideomi reaches inside his coat. You swing the chain twice over your head. Before Hideomi can pull his gun, you throw the chain. It wraps his arms tightly to his sides.

Turn to the next page.

Saito looks at you in shock. The first words out of his mouth are, "You're a *ninja!*" Then he looks from the water to the warehouse roof to Hideomi. "This whole thing was a setup?"

"A test of your loyalty," you explain. "We found two of Hideomi's men on the roof. There are probably more on the way, but we can let Detective Liu deal with them."

"So that's why you came along," Saito says to Hideomi. "To tempt me into betraying you."

"And you did!" Hideomi spits at Saito. "But don't worry—you'll never escape us."

Go on to the next page.

Detective Liu's car comes screeching onto the dock. He and two officers jump out, their pistols drawn. When they see you, they lower their guns.

"Doesn't look like you need our help," Liu comments as he slaps handcuffs on Hideomi. "Our squad cars intercepted the rest of the gang a few blocks away. They're in custody now."

Liu motions to the two officers to take Hideomi away. Again Hideomi repeats his threat to Saito. "Don't worry," Liu assures Saito. "We'll put you in a witness protection program."

Keiku and Kurt come down from the warehouse roof. They tell Liu about the other two *yakuza* in the back alley. "Any sign of the trawler?" he asks them.

They shake their heads. "I doubt there ever was one," you say. "The whole operation was to test Saito."

"And I passed with flying colors," Saito remarks sarcastically.

Liu lets his hands flop to his sides. "I guess that's it, then. Saito, you can come with us. As for the rest of you, we'll be in touch."

"Wait," Saito says, grabbing your arm. "Come with us. There's something I want to tell you."

Turn to page 17.

"No thank you," you say to the man. You start to leave, but he grabs your arm. You jerk your elbow into his ribs, and while he's momentarily stunned, you place an arm across his chest, a leg behind his knees, and sweep him across your leg. He goes crashing to the ground, and you make a quick exit.

You stalk angrily up the street, looking for a bus stop. Finally you find one. Two transfers later, you're back at the BART station.

After you've crossed the bay into Oakland, you find it's not any easier to get to The Black Dragon. The neighborhood isn't much nicer either.

The club is a crowded room full of the smell of Chinese food. Players crowd around green felt tables, shuffling what looks like domino tiles. Expensive cell phones lie on the tabletops beside the players. Money is quickly changing hands—lots of money.

Turn to the next page.

82

You ask for the manager, and moments later a stocky man in suspenders comes out counting a roll of money. You ask him about Saito. His face darkens. "You a friend of his?" he asks.

"Sort of," you say.

"Then you're not welcome here," he snaps.

"Wait, wait," you say. "Saito may be in trouble—with the *yakuza*."

"Wouldn't surprise me a bit," the manager says unhelpfully.

"Can I just check with some of the players to find out if they know anything?"

The manager looks at his watch. "I'll give you five minutes. And I'll have my eye on you the whole time."

"Thanks a lot," you murmur.

Go on to the next page.

You approach a group of middle-aged men playing at a nearby table. Describing Saito, you ask if anyone knows about him. The men just mumble and shake their heads. You try to ask more questions, but the dealer interrupts. "Listen, you want to play you pay. Otherwise, go bother someone else."

You aren't a gambler, so you nod silently and leave the table.

You don't have much luck at the other tables either. You look back at the manager, who stands at the door with his arms folded. He taps his watch. Discouraged, you leave.

The next day you try Sumioto's in the afternoon. You are still unable to get in, and the hostess claims never to have seen Saito.

You call the police. The detective assigned to the case tells you there are no new leads. "Don't worry," he adds, "we'll call you if anything comes up."

You go over to the *dojo* to ask your fellow students for help, but they can't think of what to do, and they don't seem that interested anyway.

There's nothing left to do but return to the tearoom where you and Saito first spoke. You would have gone back anyway—it still relaxes you after your *aikido* lessons. Saito does not come to the tearoom, and you imagine the worst. The *yakuza* are nasty and the Bay Area is enormous— Saito could be anywhere, in any number of places even more dangerous than the two you searched. This may just be a mystery with no solution.

The End

84

"There's no way I'm helping you die, staged or not," you tell Saito. "It's too dangerous. We've got to get out of the country."

"I'm not going back to Japan," he responds angrily.

"Fine," you say, trying to keep him calm. "I'll get a flight to Vancouver." It's the closest foreign city you can think of.

"As long as it doesn't cost more than $17.50," he shoots back, "because that's all I've got. Maybe we can catch on with a flock of Canadian geese."

Saito stalks out of the room. You're flustered. How are you going to pay for a flight?

In spite of your promise, you decide to call Nada. Your call goes through, and luckily, she answers. It's the middle of the night; her voice sounds almost like she's still asleep.

Go on to the next page.

"Nice of you to finally talk to me," you say.

"I was going to call you tomorrow," she protests sleepily.

"Listen," you say, and tell her what has happened. Five thousand miles across the ocean, you hear her wake up completely, flabbergasted by your story. She wants to hear more, but you cut her off. "I'll tell you more later. Just tell me how to get to Japan—assuming I can convince Saito to come."

"I'll call you back within the hour," Nada promises.

Turn to the next page.

86

Forty-five minutes later, your phone rings. "Here's the plan," Nada says. "A close friend of the family is in the shipping business. One of their vessels, the *Okuri*, is in port in Oakland right now. It's about to leave for the port of Yokohama, in Japan. I'll be there to meet you when it comes in."

"Which is when?" you ask.

"Three weeks, give or take a few days." When you say nothing, Nada goes on, "Ask for Captain Tanaka. He'll know what to do."

"Thanks, Nada," you say. "I knew you'd come through."

"Just go soon," Nada says. "It could leave any time in the next twelve hours."

Go on to the next page.

After you hang up the phone, though, you're not sure what to do. The only way to get Saito on the *Okuri* is to deceive him. He's dead set against going to Japan. But you know you should get him there anyway, for his own good and yours.

On the other hand, trying to trick Saito could end up in disaster. Besides, do you really want to spend three weeks on a freighter?

If you want to try to get Saito on the ship to Japan, turn to the next page.

If you think you'd better try to go to Vancouver, turn to page 93.

88

You find Saito upstairs reading your brother's graphic novels. "Get ready," you say to him. "We're leaving in five minutes."

"Where to?" he asks.

"Anywhere but here," you reply.

You go back downstairs and call a taxi. Ten minutes later, a honk comes from outside. "Let's go," you call up to Saito.

You jump into the cab and tell the driver, "Port of Oakland, Berth 83."

Saito looks at you in alarm. "I'm not getting on any boats," he exclaims. "I'll get seasick!"

"Don't worry," you say in a low voice. "It's only to Vancouver."

Go on to the next page.

The taxi drops you at the security gate to the port. "Pay the driver," you order Saito, figuring that the less money he has, the less likely he'll be to take off.

While Saito reluctantly pays, you tell the guard you're here to see Captain Tanaka of the *Okuri*. "You'd better hurry," he says. "The tugboats are coming to undock it right now."

You grab Saito's hand and run through a maze of new cars that have just been taken off another ship. Up ahead, the *Okuri* looms. It's a gigantic container ship, with a tall, straight black hull. A huge crane is loading freight containers onto the deck. The containers look like play blocks.

Turn to the next page.

You drag Saito up the gangway of the massive ship, then leave him behind on the main deck. Dodging through the galleries, you climb up deck after deck toward the bridge. You find Captain Tanaka, a white-haired man with a serene face, poring over some charts and puffing on a pipe. Breathlessly, you explain who you are and what you need.

The captain chuckles. "I think we can accommodate you. But we'll have to keep you out of sight, just to be safe."

"Fine," you say. "There's one more thing. My companion thinks we're going to Vancouver, so—"

Just then Saito comes running onto the bridge. Apparently he's been making some inquiries of his own, because he's furious. The veins pound in his neck.

"You tricked me!" he screams. "This ship's going to Yokohama, not Vancouver. Well, you can forget it. I'm not going! I'm getting off!"

"That's impossible," says Captain Tanaka, who's been issuing instructions on an intercom while you argue. "The gangway has been taken up, and the tugboats are here. We're on our way."

You don't feel anything, but when you look out the porthole, you see that the docks appear to be moving. Saito pounds his head against the bulkhead.

Saito doesn't speak to you for a whole week. Captain Tanaka has set you up in an empty container. He's even had extra furniture and cots brought in for you.

Turn to page 92.

The steward brings you three meals a day. It's quite comfortable, except for Saito's cold silence.

You're stuck inside with him all day, but at night, when things are quiet, you come out on deck. The stars overhead are brilliant and the black water churns under the ship. The seagoing life isn't so bad, you decide.

Apparently, Saito has been having similar thoughts. One night, he suddenly breaks the silence. "I'm not getting off the ship when we dock in Japan," he says. "The second mate told me I could sign on to work on the crew. We're going to Stockholm next."

You say nothing. Saito goes on, "A couple of years at sea will be good for me. It'll earn me enough money to pay off my debts. It'll give the *yakuza* a chance to forget about me. And I'll get to see the world."

"Sounds great," you say. "Except for one thing—your family. There'll be a few days' layover in Yokohama. Come with me to the *dojo*. You don't have to stay for more than a day. I know Nada can't wait to see you."

Saito looks at you as if you're crazy. His lips twitch a little, and you realize he's trying to keep from smiling. Reluctantly he agrees.

You lean against the railing and look out over the ocean. Everything suddenly seems to be working out. Saito will have a chance to make a new start and reconcile with his family. As for you, you've gotten a free trip to Japan out of the deal.

The End

You go upstairs to discuss your flight to Vancouver. "How are we going to pay for this?" you ask Saito.

Saito twirls a rubber band around his finger. "I don't know," he says slowly. His manner frightens you. Not only doesn't he know, he no longer seems to care. "Do you have a credit card?"

"No," you answer slowly, "but my parents do. Maybe I can get their number, and we can use it to buy the plane tickets."

You know it's wrong to use it without permission, but you find your parents' credit card number and buy a pair of tickets for the next flight to Vancouver. You have no idea what you're going to do when you get there, but you'll worry about that later. You can call Nada from there and let her know your change in plans.

Turn to the next page.

As it turns out, Canadian customs solves the problem for you. You haven't been in Vancouver more than five minutes when the official inspecting your passports asks you to step into his office. "Your passport's expired," he says sternly to Saito.

You sit nervously in the office while the official disappears to make inquiries. When he returns, two US Marshals are with him. "Not only is your passport expired," he says, tight-lipped, "but you're wanted for arson in San Francisco."

The Marshals escort you onto a flight back to San Francisco. When you arrive, they turn you over to a federal agent. You now have a charge of international flight added to your record.

A detective interrogates you and Saito in a closed room right there at the airport. You attempt to convince her that you're victims of the *yakuza*. Unfortunately, because you tried to flee, your credibility has been shot. You can't deny that it was your smoke bomb that set off the fire.

The detective does give you some final words of advice. "You're going to need a good lawyer," she says.

The End

96

"I don't have to do anything I don't want to," you tell Minoru, shaking your head. You have no desire to make a fool of yourself on stage.

Minoru cocks his head, smiles, and raises his glass. "To independence," he declares.

Nervously, you sip your soda. Minoru asks you questions about your family, your school, your interests. You answer without thinking, wondering how you're going to get away from him. The situation is starting to seem very weird.

Without warning, a feeling of great excitement comes over you. You feel full of energy. You decide it would be great fun to go up on stage. You manage to say something to that effect, and Minoru lets out a big laugh. "Yes, yes," he says, standing up to pull your chair back for you. For some reason, he sounds very far away.

When you get to your feet, everything changes. You feel as if you're on a merry-go-round. The noise of the bar is suddenly very loud. The room is spinning, you are whirling, and then everything goes black.

Turn to page 98.

With a bone-chilling yell, you leap from the top of the wheelhouse. You catch both men on the shoulders, knocking them to the ground. The captain gets up, aiming a fist at your face, but your lightning-fast jab to his kidneys doubles him over and a blow to his neck knocks him out.

"Hold it!" Iwata says. You whirl to see him aiming a pistol at your heart. "We should have gotten rid of you a long time ago," he snarls.

Suddenly his head snaps, and he falls forward to the deck. Debbie stands behind him, holding the butt of the pistol, which has just been applied to the side of Iwata's skull. She looks at the gun curiously.

"Thanks," you say.

Suddenly Simon shows up, clapping you and Debbie on the back and congratulating you. The three of you drag the captain and Iwata below and get the whole lot of them locked up in the brig.

Debbie takes the helm. Simon finds the radio and sends out a Mayday. The Coast Guard responds, saying help is on the way.

The seas are quiet, and all of you sit back to enjoy the vacation Minoru had promised. You're still not sure what happened to Saito, but you've bagged yourself a band of *yakuza*. You can only hope that when the police investigate, they'll turn up your new potential friend.

The End

98

When you wake up, you find that you're in a small room. There is a futon mattress on the floor, a glass of water on a stand next to it, and four white walls. The door to the room is small but made of metal. You try the handle. The door does not budge a millimeter. You check for your *ninja* tools. They're gone.

You lie back down on the futon and try to think but you become drowsy again and drift away.

The next time you wake up, you're being shaken by Minoru. A broad smile is on his face. He holds a plate of fish and rice. "Time to eat," he says, offering the food.

You just glare at him. "Where am I? I want to leave."

Minoru gives you another one of his syrupy smiles. "We will leave soon," he assures you. "We'll travel the sea. A fun trip!"

"What are you talking about?" you demand.

"You have the chance to visit an exotic place," Minoru says in a smooth tone. "Don't worry, we'll pay all your expenses."

You don't like the sound of this at all. Once again you demand to know what is going on.

Minoru goes to the door. "You will find out soon enough," he says. "Let's just say you'll be helping us out a great deal, and we'll show our appreciation."

He takes a small velvet box from his pocket. "An item with great value to us is inside this box. When you reach the destination, you will carry it through customs for us. Then your job will be done, and you'll reap your reward."

Turn to page 100.

100

"I don't want a reward! I don't want anything to do with this!"

His eyes become hard. "But you do. It is far more pleasant than ending up at the bottom of the bay wrapped in chains."

The door clicks shut behind Minoru. You hear a bolt being locked. Now you're sure that something very bad is happening. Minoru wants you to smuggle an item worth a lot of money into another country. He or his men would draw the attention of customs agents, but you're much less likely to be questioned.

The more you think about Minoru's words and his smug, slimy manner, the angrier you get. How dare he do this to you? You have realized by now that he put something in your drink back at the club, then he locked you up in this cubicle. Now he's planning to take you across the ocean and use you as a courier for some kind of black market operation.

Your blood boils. You want to kick down the walls. Testing them out, you can tell they're pretty flimsy—just some plaster and wood. You could destroy them with a few kicks. You're tempted to do it. If nothing else, it will teach Minoru a lesson.

If you decide to kick through the walls, turn to page 102.

If you decide not to demonstrate your power just yet, turn to page 117.

"No waiting!" you decide. "Let's strike now. Come on!"

You lead the charge out of the cabin. Debbie follows you, inspecting the pistol. Simon falls in behind her, but at a safe distance.

A spiral staircase appears to lead up to the deck. "Let's go and stir up some trouble," you say. "I'll climb first, and you two come up in 60 seconds. Debbie, you don't have to actually use the gun—just pretend you will."

You bound up the steps and break out onto the deck, ready for anything. A grizzled deckhand looks at you curiously. You fell him with a single blow to the solar plexus. Two more come running at you. You jump high in the air, flooring each of them with a kick. Then a voice behind you barks, "Stop! Stop right there!"

You whirl to see the captain with the first mate, Iwata, each holding a pistol. You put up your hands, hoping Debbie will arrive soon. She does, poking her head out the hatchway behind the captain. "Hold!" she says, taking aim with the pistol.

Turn to page 39.

102

You're going to kick down these walls just as soon as you know Minoru has left.

You wait half an hour. Finally, it's quiet outside. You choose a spot in the wall between two studs. Then you back up.

With three steps you deliver a flying double-heel kick to the wall, smashing in a hole the size of a basketball. It's incredibly satisfying. You proceed with a blinding series of kicks and punches, destroying a space in the wall large enough for your body to fit through. Plaster dust flies all over the place.

You still have to deal with the plaster on the other side of the studs, but you don't waste time with more kicks. You simply attack it with three powerful head-butts. On the third one, the wall crumbles, and you break through, falling forward into the next room.

Coughing and partially blinded, you clear your eyes just in time to see several burly men waiting for you. You have no chance against them. Three hold you down while another runs to get Minoru. You try every trick you know, but the *yakuza* are just too strong.

Minoru appears a few minutes later with a needle and syringe. "Tsk, tsk," he says. "It appears our guest doesn't want to take the luxury trip we have planned. Well, we have another package for obstinate tourists like you. You'll still be taking a sea trip. But under it, not over! Ha ha ha!"

The last thing you remember is the needle plunging into your arm.

Turn to page 104.

When you come to, all is dark. You use your other senses to take stock. You're rolling back and forth and an auto engine rumbles beneath you. You feel around and realize you're inside some kind of canvas bag, lying flat. The floor underneath you is hard and ribbed. A van, and you're in the back of it. But where is it going?

You feel around inside the canvas and find a zipper. Working your finger into the top of it, you manage to open it a few inches. Still nothing but darkness.

The van stops. The back doors open and the scent of salt water comes to your nose.

"Unload these crates," a voice commands.

You hear the scraping of wood beside you. As the crates are being removed from around you, the commanding voice comes again. "Saito, after you're done, get the forklift."

"Yes, Hideomi."

Saito! You dare to open an eye again and lift up an inch to peer out. Industrial lights illuminate a pier. The gang must be moving the crates onto a ship. And Saito is working with them!

Hideomi approaches, and you quickly play dead. He touches the canvas bag in which you're contained and says, "And get some chains to wrap up this package."

Footsteps move away. You take a gamble they belong to Hideomi. "Psst! Saito!" you hiss, sitting up to open the bag more. "I need help!"

Go on to the next page.

"Huh?" he says, surprised. He looks into the van and lets out a gasp. "What—what are you doing here?"

"I was going to ask you the same thing. I'm not here by choice."

"Me neither, but..."

"At least untie me," you insist.

Saito hurriedly works at your knots. "I'm taking a big risk," he mutters.

"Get the forklift, like your boss said."

You jump out of the van and pry open one of the crates. You're startled by what you find—it's packed full of handguns!

The whining engine of the forklift approaches a few minutes later. You're not sure what Saito's intentions are, but now is the time to put him to the test.

Turn to the next page.

You take four guns out of the crate you've opened. When Saito arrives behind the controls of the forklift, you motion him over and hand him two of the guns.

Saito looks at you in disbelief. "Are you insane?"

You give him a hard stare. "Whose side are you on anyway?"

"My own," he mutters, but he takes the guns. You help him load the crates onto the fork, leaving a space for yourself behind them. You climb onto the forks and motion Saito to back out.

Saito raises the fork with you hidden behind the crates, backs the machine away from the van, and drives to the edge of the dock. You peer over a crate. Unfortunately, at that very moment one of the *yakuza* is looking straight at you.

Turn to page 108.

"Run!" you yell to Saito, your feet pounding the pavement. He looks at you with anger, and dodges off in the opposite direction.

As soon as you begin running, you realize you've made a terrible mistake. The *yakuza* did not pick this location because it had lots of routes out for potential getaways. In less than a minute, three men you hadn't seen capture you, and they drag Saito over beside you.

"Live as traitors, die as traitors," Hideomi says to you both.

The End

108

"Freeze!" you say, climbing up on top of the crates, a gun in each hand. Only you know that they're empty of ammunition.

You survey the dock. All motion has stopped. There are a lot more *yakuza* here than you expected. Each one of them has a hand poised inside his jacket.

Saito jumps off the forklift seat. He aims his guns. "Tell them to throw out their weapons, Hideomi," Saito says.

Hideomi looks at him defiantly. "Go ahead and kill me, Saito. You know I'd rather die than surrender to a punk like you."

Go on to the next page.

Then everything seems to happen at once. Several of Hideomi's men pull their guns. You take cover behind the crates. You turn the guns in your hand around and, grasping the barrels between your thumb and forefinger, stand up and sling them like *shuriken* at two of the *yakuza*, knocking the guns from their hands.

Out of the corner of your eye, to your amazement, you see Saito do the same thing. You climb on top of the crates and gauge the distance to the water beyond the edge of the dock.

You're outnumbered if you decide to run for it. The only other choice you can see is to dive into the cold water of the bay and hope for the best.

If you run for it, turn to page 107.

If you dive into the bay, turn to page 111.

"Dive!" you yell, taking the leap and plunging into the cold water. Saito splashes in beside you, and together you swim as fast as you can underwater. When you surface, bullets are zinging into the water all around you. You see a small sailboat tied up nearby, and point to it.

"Swim to the boat!" you yell to Saito.

The two of you reach the boat quickly and pull yourselves over the gunwale. Splintered wood flies as bullets ricochet off the hull. Keeping low, you untie the boat and push away from the dock. Saito raises the sail. As usual, there is a strong breeze on the bay, and you zoom away.

The sail is full of bullet holes, but it still catches the wind. You look back to see the *yakuza* untying a boat and backing away from the dock. It's a much larger craft, though, and is slow to get started.

Turn to the next page.

112

Saito is at the rudder. The boat is tacking wildly. You jump back and forth from port to starboard as it shifts direction. "You're doing a great job," you assure Saito.

He laughs. "I've never done this before in my life."

A big tanker looms ahead. You motion Saito to cut in front of it. A horn bellows from the tanker, but you just make it through. You turn and watch the enormous prow of the ship go by overhead.

You try to relax a little—the tanker is hiding you from the *yakuza* boat. If you can keep the big ship between the two of you, you may be able to escape.

Suddenly, you notice that there are two inches of water sloshing at your feet. The bullets have turned your boat into a sieve!

Saito notices it too. "I hope you're a good swimmer," you say.

Go on to the next page.

The sailboat is sinking quickly, but luck seems to be with you today. Angel Island, which sits in the middle of the bay, is only a quarter mile away. You and Saito take off your shoes and abandon ship.

You swim hard for the island. Looking back, you see that the sailboat has sunk without a trace. The tanker still hides you from the *yakuza*. They'll have no idea what became of you.

By the time you and Saito pull yourselves ashore on Angel Island, the *yakuza* boat is nowhere to be seen. You take cover up in some trees just to be safe, but you figure they'll keep searching for the sailboat. For now, you can lie low and take a ferry back to the city later on.

Turn to the next page.

114

Exhausted, you sit shivering under a eucalyptus tree. Now you have a chance to ask Saito the question that's been on your mind for over an hour. "So you're a *ninja*," you say point-blank.

Saito can't suppress his smile. "You too," he says. "But I'm not surprised. Once I heard you studied with the Kurayama family, I expected as much."

"And you?" you ask.

You have to lean very close to hear Saito murmur, "I, too, am a Kurayama."

You look at him in shock. He proceeds to tell you a long story about how he came to be here. He was part of the respected Kurayama family of Japan, first cousin to your friend Nada. But he disgraced himself by selling his services as a *ninja* and decided to leave Japan for San Francisco. Falling on hard times, he got involved in gambling and had to borrow money from the *yakuza*. When he couldn't pay it back, they forced him to join their ranks. That's how he came to help them smuggle guns—among other things—out of the city.

"Perhaps it's time to go back to your family," you say quietly.

"Yes," he says, "I think maybe it is."

The End

You decide to save your anger for a better target. The plate of food Minoru has left tempts you. You have to admit you're pretty hungry.

It doesn't occur to you until after you're done eating that the food might have been drugged, like your drink at the club. It's too late—that familiar feeling of sleepiness is coming over you again.

The next thing you know you're swaying back and forth, suspended in midair. You try to move your arms and legs, but you can't. You pop open one eye, but immediately close it. You glimpsed a violet dragon with big fangs, but that was enough. The dragon was a tattoo, rippling on the biceps of a *yakuza*. You're all trussed up and being carried down a flight of stairs like a sack of potatoes.

You're pretty sure they didn't see you open your eye. You pretend to be unconscious as they take you out a door. The men start to swing you back and forth as if they're going to toss you. Then you hear Minoru's voice.

"Careful with the ambassador!" he barks. The men chuckle and set you down inside some kind of compartment. Then a car door slams shut.

Turn to the next page.

118

You're in the trunk of a car, being carried up and down the hills of San Francisco. Minoru's men have tied you up well and you can't escape their bonds.

The road flattens and the car comes to stop. When the trunk opens, you see four large men in sleeveless t-shirts, their bulging arm and shoulder muscles covered with tattoos, coming to lift you out. Trussed up as you are, there's not much you can do about it.

Minoru appears again, like a bad dream. He's got a syringe. The men hold you still while he injects it into your arm. You slide into unconsciousness again.

Turn to page 120.

120

When you come to, you feel awful. Your head is pounding, and it seems like your body weighs about three hundred pounds. You try to stand up, but the room is rocking back and forth. Dizzy and weak at the knees, you lie back down.

You realize two sets of eyes are upon you. You find yourself on a tiny bunk in a narrow cabin. Through a porthole, you see the blue horizon line of the ocean rising and falling. You're on a ship!

As your fellow passengers come into focus, you realize they are kids, a boy with dark hair and a girl who is blonde. The boy runs to a corner and throws up. The girl sits down next to you. "Are you all right?" she asks.

You nod weakly and look over at the boy. "Poor Simon," the girl says. "He's been doing that all trip. My name's Debbie."

"How long have we been out to sea?" you ask.

"Just a couple of days. We've got a long voyage in front of us."

"Where are we going?" you ask.

The girl shrugs. "Hong Kong, probably. But they don't tell us much."

Go on to the next page.

"Why Hong Kong?"

The girl looks at you curiously. "Don't you know?" she says. "We're vehicles. No one will think we might be helping a smuggling ring."

You remember the velvet box. "Jewels?"

"You might say that. There are extremely rare ancient artifacts, the kind that should be in a museum or monastery, gems with incredible powers, and stones that are said to have been used back in the days of the legendary *tengu*."

Turn to the next page.

122

"*Tengu*," you whisper. You encountered the fabulous beings in your previous adventures with Nada. They are said to have first taught the *ninja* their arts. "What are these guys doing with the gems? Selling them to the highest bidder, I suppose."

Debbie nods. Simon, done with throwing up, stands beside her.

"If only we could get our hands on them…" you say.

"First Mate Iwata, Minoru's man in charge, keeps them locked away. Minoru took a flight and will meet us at the port. When the time comes, as we approach the customs checkpoint, he'll give a small box to each of us. We go through one at a time. A man of his will be waiting on the other side. If one of us tries to betray him, he'll have the other two of us killed. And the betrayer is not likely to survive either."

"So our fates are intertwined," Simon says. "I don't see much choice. If we go through with it, there's a chance they'll let us go."

"When we can identify them?" you say. "I doubt it. We need to do something before we get into port."

"Take it easy," Simon says. "Maybe the police will be waiting when we get there. You sound like trouble. No wonder they put you out cold."

"I'm not taking anything easy. Right now, we have the advantage of surprise. I know a few things the *tengu* once taught."

Go on to the next page.

Simon scoffs, but Debbie says, "I grew up on a ranch. My parents taught me how to hunt. I know a few things too."

"Give me a break, you two," Simon replies. "What chance do we have against these guys?"

"We'll find out soon enough," you say. Someone is unlocking the hatch to the cabin. All eyes are on you as you go to the door.

Turn to the next page.

124

As soon as the door opens and you see a hand, you grab it. You twist it over your back and flip the hand's owner over the top. He lands with a big thud and doesn't move.

You stare at the unconscious man. Simon's eyes are wide with fear. You pat the man's pockets and remove a pistol. Handing it to Debbie, you say, "Are you with me?"

She takes the gun and turns it over in her hands. "Yes," she says, "but—"

"But what?" you demand. "Let's get moving before they realize their friend is missing."

"I think we should go slow," Debbie says. "Wait until another guy comes down. That way we can get them one by one."

"What are we going to do?" Simon cries at you. "We have to do something! Hurry!"

But Debbie, with her hunter's instincts, might have a point. Taking the smuggling crew down one by one might be a better strategy.

If you want to lead an attack now, turn to page 101.

If you decide to wait for the next smuggler, go on to the next page.

"You're right, Debbie," you say. "Let's wait for the next smuggler. This doesn't seem like a very big ship. There probably aren't many more of them."

You close the door and drag the unconscious man into the cabin. After you and Debbie tear up sheets to tie the man up, the two of you quietly set up a plan. Simon sits off to the side, sulking.

A few minutes later, you hear a man's voice outside the door. It sounds like he's calling for his crewmate. Debbie and Simon return to their bunks. Silently you wait behind the door. The man pushes it open and steps inside. You rise behind him and give him a vicious strike to the neck.

"Two down," Debbie says, dragging him in.

"But how many to go?" you wonder.

You stop two more smugglers the same way. As Debbie starts to bind and gag the fourth man, you motion to her to wait. "He's still conscious," you say. "Let's see if we can get some information."

Once the man recovers his wits, you lean down and ask, "How many more of you are there?"

The *yakuza* glares at you and says something you're glad you don't understand. You grab one of his fingers and apply a *ninja* twist. He howls. "Just the captain and Iwata," he says when you let go.

You look up at Debbie. "I think it's time to make our move."

"Right," she says. "As soon as we get this guy tied up."

Turn to the next page.

Leaving Simon to watch over the tied-up men, you and Debbie head above deck. She still has the pistol.

"Are you willing to act as bait?" you ask as you steal up the spiral staircase leading to the wheelhouse.

Go on to the next page.

"As long as you keep doing the dirty work," she answers.

"Give me about a minute," you say. "Then go up and call the captain and Iwata. Stand just inside the door—but don't go in too far. I hope they're both together."

Silently, you creep up the last of the spiral staircase and poke your head out on deck. All seems quiet. Keeping low, you scamper the length of the boat. In a flash, you climb up on top of the wheelhouse, making hardly a sound.

Debbie appears below, at the door to the wheelhouse. Holding the pistol in front of her, she cautiously takes a step forward, then calls in, "Hey you sleazeballs! Guess what, I'm hijacking this boat!"

A man's head appears just below you. "What's this, a mutiny?" he chuckles.

"That's right, Captain," Debbie says. She raises the gun.

The captain calls over his shoulder, "Hey, Iwata, come on over here. Our cargo is getting brave!"

Iwata's head comes into view. "Now, let's see how serious you are about this mutiny," the captain says to Debbie.

"You don't really want to pull that trigger, do you?" Iwata adds.

The two men advance on her. She takes a step back, looking worried.

Turn to page 97.

GLOSSARY

Aikido – Ai: "harmony"; ki: "energy"; do: "the way." A defensive practice using pivoting motions and the momentum of the attacker to neutralize an attack.

Bujutsu – A term to describe many Japanese warrior arts.

Dojo – The place were martial arts are practiced.

Gin – Obligation.

Girt – Loyalty.

Kaginawa – A grapple or hook attached to the end of a rope.

Karate – Literally, "empty-handed." A martial art utilizing punches and kicks.

Kimono – A robe-like garment, usually cotton or silk, worn by men and women.

Kusari-fundo – *Ninja* weapon, a length of chain with weights at either end.

Metsubishi – *Ninja* blinding powder, used to temporarily cloud the vision of an opponent.

Nihonmachi – Another name for Japantown in San Francisco.

Ninja – A person adept at the art of *ninjutsu*.

Ninjutsu – The "art of stealth" or "way of invisibility." An unconventional discipline incorporating martial arts, special weapons, techniques of concealment, and sorcery.

Oya-bun – The leader or boss of a *yakuza* clan.

Pai Gow – A Chinese game that can either be played with cards or dominoes. *Pai Gow* is traditionally played with dominoes but can also be played as a version of poker with playing cards.

Samurai – Japanese feudal warrior. The *samurai* were the highest class, followed by farmers, craftsmen, and finally merchants. *Samurai* were also the administrators of the state.

Sensei – Master, teacher.

Seppuku – Ritual suicide, an honorable form of death for *samurai*.

Shuriken – A metal throwing blade, often star shaped.

Tengu – Mythical creatures supposed to have first taught *ninja* their art. Sometimes portrayed as helpful but mischievous, other times as devilish, *tengu* are often shown with long noses or beaks, wings attached to the body of an old man, and long claws or fingernails. They wear capes of feathers or leaves, live in trees in the mountains, and, according to one description, are the condensed spirit of the principle of *yin*, or darkness.

Yakuza – A gangster. A member of an organized criminal gang.

Yubitsume – The act or ritual of cutting off the first joint of one's pinky finger as a sign of loyalty to one's boss. It can also be performed as an act of apology as well as punishment.

ABOUT THE ARTISTS

Illustrator: Suzanne Nugent received her BFA in illustration from Moore College of Art & Design in Philadelphia, Pennsylvania. She now resides with her husband, Fred, in Philadelphia and works as a freelance illustrator. She first discovered her love for *Choose Your Own Adventure*® books when she was only four years old, which inspired her to become an artist.

Cover Artist: Gabhor Utomo was born in Indonesia. He moved to California to pursue his passion in art. He received his degree from Academy of Art University in San Francisco in spring 2003. Since graduation, he's worked as a freelance illustrator and has illustrated a number of children's books. Gabhor lives with his wife, Dina, and his twin girls in the San Francisco Bay area.

ABOUT THE AUTHOR

JAY LEIBOLD was born in Denver, Colorado. Jay has written *Secret of the Ninja, Sabotage, Grand Canyon Odyssey, Spy For George Washington, Return of the Ninja, The Search for Aladdin's Lamp, You are a Millionaire, Beyond the Great Wall, Revenge of the Russian Ghost, Surf Monkeys,* and *Ninja Cyborg* in the *Choose Your Own Adventure®* series.

For games, activities, and other fun stuff, or to write to Chooseco, visit us online at CYOA.com

The History of Gamebooks

Although the *Choose Your Own Adventure* series, first published in 1976, may be the best known example of gamebooks, it was not the first.

In 1941, the legendary Argentine writer Jorge Luis Borges published *Examen de la obra de Herbert Quain* or *An Examination of the Work of Herbert Quain,* a short story that contained three parts and nine endings. He followed that with his better known work, *El jardín de senderos que se bifurcan,* or *The Garden of Forking Paths,* a novel about a writer lost in a garden

Jorge Luis Borges maze that had multiple story lines and endings.

More than 20 years later, in 1964, another famous Argentine writer, Julio Cortázar, published a novel called *Rayuela* or *Hopscotch.* This book was composed of 155 "chapters" and the reader could make  Julio Cortázar their way through a number of different "novels" depending on choices they made. At the same time, French author Raymond Queneau wrote an interactive story entitled *Un conte à votre façon,* or *A Story As You Like It.*

Early in the 1970s, a popular series for children called *Trackers* was published in the UK that contained multiple choices and endings. In 1976,

Journey Under the Sea, 1st Edition

R. A. Montgomery wrote and published the first gamebook for young adults: *Journey Under the Sea* under the series name *The Adventures of You*. This was changed to *Choose Your Own Adventure* by Bantam Books when they published this and five others to launch the series in 1979. The success of CYOA spawned many imitators and the term gamebooks came into use to refer to any books that utilized the second person "you" to tell a story using multiple choices and endings.

Montgomery said in an interview in 2013: "This wasn't traditional literature. The *New York Times* children's book reviewer called *Choose Your Own Adventure* a literary movement. Indeed it was. The most important thing for me has always been to get kids reading. It's not the format, it's not even the writing. The reading happened because kids were in the driver's seat. They were the mountain climber, they were the doctor, they were the deep-sea explorer. They made choices, and so they read. There were people who expressed the feeling that nonlinear literature wasn't 'normal.' But interactive books have a long history, going back 70 years."

Young R. A. Montgomery

Choose Your Own Adventure Timeline

1977 – R. A. Montgomery writes *Journey Under the Sea* under the pen name Robert Mountain. It is published by Vermont Crossroads Press along with the title *Sugar Cane Island* under the series name *The Adventures of You*.

1979 – Montgomery brings his book series to New York where it is rejected by 14 publishers before being purchased by Bantam Books for the brand new children's division. The new series is renamed *Choose Your Own Adventure*.

1980 – *Space and Beyond* initial sales are slow until Bantam seeds libraries across the U. S. with 100,000 free copies.

1983 – CYOA sales reach ten million units of the first 14 titles.

1984 – For a six week period, 9 spots of the top 15 books on the Waldenbooks Children's Bestsellers list belong to CYOA. *Choose* dominates the list throughout the 1980s.

1989 – Ten years after its original publication, over 150 CYOA titles have been published.

1990 – R. A. Montgomery publishes the *TRIO* series with Bantam, a six-book series that draws inspiration from future worlds in CYOA titles *Escape* and *Beyond Escape*.

1992 – ABC TV adapts Shannon Gilligan's CYOA title *The Case of the Silk King* as a made-for-TV movie. It is set in Thailand and stars Pat Morita, Soleil Moon Frye and Chad Allen.

1995 – A horror trend emerges in the children's book market, and Bantam launches *Choose Your Own Nightmare*, a series of shorter CYOA titles focused on creepy themes. The subseries is translated into several languages and converted to DVD and computer games.

1998 – Bantam licenses property from *Star Wars* to release *Choose Your Own Star Wars Adventures*. The 3-book series features traditional CYOA elements to place the reader in each of the existing *Star Wars* films and feature holograms on the covers.

2003 – With the series virtually out of print, the copyright licenses and the *Choose Your Own Adventure* trademark revert to R. A. Montgomery. He forms Chooseco LLC with Shannon Gilligan.

2005 – *Choose Your Own Adventure* is re-launched into the education market, with all new art and covers. Texts have been updated to reflect changes to technology and discoveries in archaeology and science.

2006 – Chooseco LLC, operating out of a renovated farmhouse in Waitsfield, Vermont, publishes the series for the North American retail market, shipping 900,000 copies in its first six months.

2008 – Chooseco publishes CYOA *The Golden Path*, a three volume epic for readers 10+, written by Anson Montgomery.

2008 – Poptropica and Chooseco partner to develop the first branded Poptropica island, "Nabooti Island" based on CYOA #4, *The Lost Jewels of Nabooti*.

2009 – *Choose Your Own Adventure* celebrates 30 years in print and releases two titles in partnership with WADA, the World Anti-Doping Agency, to emphasize fairness in sport.

2010 – Chooseco launches a new look for the classic books using special neon ink.

2013 – Chooseco launches eBooks on Kindle and in the iBookstore with trackable maps and other bonus features. The project is briefly hung up when Apple has to rewrite its terms and conditions for publishers to create space for this innovative eBook type.

2014 – Brazil and Korea license publishing rights to the series. 20 foreign publishers currently distribute the series worldwide.

2014 – Beloved series founder R. A. Montgomery dies at age 78. He finishes his final book in the *Choose Your Own Adventure* series only weeks before.

2018 – Z-Man Games releases the first-ever Choose Your Own Adventure board game, adapted from *House of Danger*. Record sales lead to the creation of a new game for 2019 based on *War with the Evil Power Master*.

2019 – Chooseco publishes a new sub-series of Choose Your Own Adventure books based on real-life spies. The first two of the series are *Spies: Mata Hari* and *Spies: James Armistead Lafayette*, by debut authors Katherine Factor and Kyandreia Jones.

2019 – The first-ever *Choose Your Own Adventure* audiobooks are released, with voice-activated interactive technology. These audiobooks include *Journey Under the Sea*, *The Abominable Snowman*, *The Magic of the Unicorn*, and more.

THE LOST NINJA

This book is different from other books.

You and YOU ALONE are in charge of what happens in this story.

There are dangers, choices, adventures, and consequences. YOU must use all of your numerous talents and much of your enormous intelligence. The wrong decision could end in disaster—even death. But don't despair. At any time, YOU can go back and make another choice, alter the path of your story, and change its result.

After living and studying in Japan for two years at your friend Nada's *dojo*, you are now living in Oakland, California. You continue to study *ninjutsu* at a local *dojo*, feeling at home and as if you are back in Japan. One day, everything changes when a fellow *aikido* classmate, Saito, runs into you and begins asking you odd questions at the Haiku Tearoom in Japantown. When Saito suddenly gets thrown into a car and all you are left with is a piece of paper with the name of a lounge, you realize you have an important choice to make! Do you utilize your *ninja* training and try to find Saito yourself, OR do you decide to let the police handle it? Good luck!

VISIT US ONLINE AT WWW.CYOA.COM